PARABLES IRONIC
AND GROTESQUE

Douglas G. Campbell

Oblique Voices Press | Portland, Oregon

PARABLES IRONIC AND GROTESQUE

Copyright © 2020 Douglas G. Campbell

ISBN-13: 978-0-9984446-2-8

VOICES PRESS

9310 SW 18th Pl
Portland, OR 97219

About the Author:

Douglas G. Campbell lives in Portland, Oregon. He is Professor Emeritus of art at George Fox University where he taught painting, printmaking, drawing and art history courses. His poetry and artworks have been published in a number of periodicals, and his artwork is represented in collections such as The Portland Art Museum, Oregon State University, Ashforth Pacific, Inc. and George Fox University.

The stories in this book were written throughout the years before his stroke in 2012, which subsequently left him with a language disorder called aphasia. This book reflects the process of reengaging with his former writing and also encouraging him to share his work with the world.

For my wife, Rebecca and my sons, Joshua and Ian.

Table of Contents

Foreword

At this point in my life, it is my pleasure to have a near-weekly luncheon date with the author of this book, Doug Campbell. It is ironic to be writing this introduction and not speaking it over the table at lunch, in our now broke-speech idiom. I used to have long conversations with Doug, sometimes on wonderful hikes in the Cascade Mountains. Now our walks seem to be in a large grocery store, he looking for diet Pepsi and I for some more local vintage. The book he has now released is a series of stories I will simply list by name each story, and comment upon each, always with an eye to the Ironic and Grotesque in our lives, as if reminisced as old men over lunch. Please forgive my stream of consciousness writing as I react to each story as I experienced it.

Blood

Doug's humor and irony are reminiscent of a television show that I could guess both he and I were raised with, *The Twilight Zone*. His stories remind me of some stories some of my old friends now tell me today, unfortunately with absolutely no sense of irony in the telling. Sometimes irony, somewhere besides the political arena please God, could help us all connect our privileged existence to the ground, in this story's case, the bloody floor of our existence upon which we stand. Using Doug's pun-parlance, the floor of our existence would be the "first-story" of our existence.

Then again, some people might say Doug has a slightly "glass half full" view of the world. I'm just saying.

Though he did hail from Florida, he's no huckster. He couldn't sell you a proverbial piece of swampland.

The Fool and the Wall
Ancient proverbs were collected and refined, some of them riddles and parables, for the purpose of making fools wise, if they would come to see or hear. I sometimes despair that our current political discourse, dripping as it does with irony, simply provokes bile, to little effect. There is responsibility to one who would use irony, for the author to be found within the story themselves, not sitting above upon a cloud. Doug stands in a recent tradition. Modern proverbs written as short stories and novels, have a deep tradition of irony, morbidity and sublimity, the best of times, the worst of times. What the Dickens?

Road Kill
Here is a story that is timely, given our environmental and species crises. Unlike our current technophiles, there seems to be no quick fix, or perhaps the fix comes in pharmaceutical prescription form. You tell me.

Peace
This story is a meditation on the irony of frequent greetings of "peace" or "peace be with you," and the inner haunting that it just isn't so. It exemplifies the inward dialogical style of this author, told in the first-person narrator voice, that gives interpretation to the "outer world," in disquieting ways.

Thirst
This story is quite psychological, or is it? We meet a character with almost no introduction, development, and almost archetypal in quality. She seems like ancient wisdom personified (Proverbs), or the quality of mercy itself. Like so much else in life that is good, she must be welcomed freely, not grasped; right there to be taken, yet slips through our fingers.

Interview by Donald Wrymouth
This story marks a change in genre, and is written in the form of a play, many times, on words. The words, "sham and a mockery of a sham," are first to come to mind. Although irony, a theme of this book, is found in its first pages, much of the feel in earlier stories in this book are 19th-Century.   In this story we seem to catapult into the 21st-Century. In it, Doug, himself a well-respected artist and faculty member wrote of the kinds of conversations within the academic and artistic community, that through artifice and double-speak, threaten the very plausibility of discussion at all. It is not sarcastic speech, it approaches hyperbolic balderdashery!!! It is as if the art universe folded back upon itself and waved like a flag in the wind. It is raucous mad-hattery at its best and irreverent fracking under the academic world at its worst.

Sleeping Through the Apocalypse and other Unpleasant Occurrences
In this story, we are presented with the problematic nature of human consciousness in the post-modern world, specifically the problem of what constitutes reality, in philosophy-speak, the tableness of tables. At the very least, what is it like when what for centu-

ries we have referred to as the "natural world" infringes upon the manufactured electronic-mediated cosmos. This story illustrates the fundamental difficulty of having a real conversation about the very destruction of the cosmos, when we are not convinced it even exists in our experience any more. That's not irony Doug, that's nightmare, and you can quote Edgar Allen Poe, and quoth ravens and all, but its just dark. And don't tell me you don't know what you're doing. You're an artist and you know about light and dark and seeing. You know just what you are doing. It is when Plato's caveman meets Vana White and chooses to enter the real world through door number two. I am reminded of the recent commercial on TV, where the suburban woman confronts some urban youth through her front-door camera, "Hey, what are you knuckle-heads doing on my front lawn?" She, herself, hasn't been there in years, it's just too threatening. By focusing on youth on her lawn, through her camera lens, she can forget that her front yard is warming up. This story of Doug's ends with the line, "We live in a soulless world with out the least scrap of justice." Well, Doug, so much for irony. So much for art. Why don't you just say it?

The Great Birdhouse
This story is a parable. Here we see the true nature of parable. By speaking too plainly and without the cloak of deniability, if for example, one was to say, "the emperor has no clothes," at first one is derided, but there is much further danger. Here we come to grips with the irony of this book as an artifact of Doug's life. Doug was a professor at a Christian college, or as he might say ironically, a Christian univer-

sity, at the time he wrote this book or this collection. People there would sometimes say, WWJD, or What Would Jesus Do. I wonder, just now, WWGOS, What Would George Orwell Say? In previous work, Doug has dabbled in Animal Farm, but here we are confronted with 1984 for artists. What is it like to have a university where capitalism becomes the heart and soul, the ideology, and where everything is run by social scientists with clipboards and lab coats? There is a risk of the lights going dim and art mouldering in an attic. As university, so society?

The irony of this artifact, this book, is the irony of how we communicate with each other in post-speak society. In the cyber-world, I can send off a message, and a few seconds later someone else speaks back to me or at me with a tweet, but usually there is a time interval between parts of the same message. Alexander Graham Bell's first message on the telephone, "Mr. Watson –come here– I want to see you," was instantaneous and continuous. Cyber-communication is discontinuous, disjunctive, and in that sense ironic. Here we are just now getting around to reading a book by Doug Campbell, written when he was a great speaker, when his voice was in the moment, some years ago before his stroke. Given his current difficulty in saying words, it is ironic to read such prescient work written about our society. I hope to have lunch with Doug again in days, and our conversation will be halting, frustrating, even primitive. But here I read him with such thoughtful and deft clarity. Doug loves puns, like his painting of a frog workshop, titled "toad's tools." This book is filled with puns. I hope Doug will forgive me for my pun, quite in bad taste, but written with deepest empathy, I weep as I write it, that this book reads like "a stroke of genius."

Jay Beaman, PhD

Blood

It was not a deep cut. There was not really much blood oozing from my right wrist. Yet there was enough pain that it was hard to ignore the wound. It had happened when I had reached inside the news box for a paper. I did not really need to buy the paper, for I would find another at my office when I returned there. But a photograph on the front page had caught my attention. Though the quality was poor, it was clear that my boyhood friend had done something, at least enough to get her image on the front page. But as I pulled the paper from the news box the inside of my wrist was caught momentarily by the latch. A sharp projection had scraped, somewhat tragically, through my skin, just deep enough to draw blood. And wouldn't you just know, red blotches were spreading across her face and the print below it. I must find a pharmacy.

Soon I found a pharmacy and with some gauze and tape had stanched the flow. But now, on the cuff of my shirt, there was an unsightly stain and several dark reddish-brown blotches were visible upon my wool trousers. Another trip to that wretch the dry cleaner would be needed. He was the only dry cleaner in my area, so I had no choice but to take my cleaning to him. But he never had things ready on time. Rotten luck, this whole business. I must find a bench on which to sit now that the bleeding had stopped.

In a few minutes I was there in the park at the crossing of St. Mary's Road and the Johnstown Pike. It was one of my least favorite parks. There were few trees and children had trodden all the grass down to dust. The place was bleak and unsightly, but it was the closest park and there were two benches, though both were rusted and ugly with pigeon droppings.

I found a small clean area and sat down to find out what it was she had done. Oh, so she had become a missionary. Yes, yes, I remember that was her intention. Spent all her time reading those books about women doctors in China and other ungodly places. Guess she thought she could save the lives of those miserable heathen. I read quickly the four brief paragraphs.

She was dead from an outbreak of cholera. After twenty-five years as a physician she had earned nothing but death. And who cared? Surely it was nice, I guess, to get one's photo in the paper for doing good. But soon she would sink into oblivion and nobody would remember her.

And she had had such promise. Yes, she had been beautiful when I had known her in school. But now, if the blurred and bloody photo was at all close to the truth, she had lived a rough life, and for what? Tired eyes sunk in deeply, hair pulled back tightly, and a soiled white physicians smock were her legacy. Yes, yes I was angry, for I had asked her to marry me. How wonderful it would have been. She could have practiced medicine while I went about my business. But she had turned me down, gone off to medical school, and I had not heard from her again, except that one time. What nerve she had, to ask me for financial support for her missionary work. She picked some rat hole in Africa, not me. Let her suffer there if she chose, but I would not pay for it. I did not deign to answer. I had crumpled her letter and thrown it into the stove to burn.

Enough of this, I must get back to my office. I had a client to meet at 2:00 p.m. and must put on a fresh shirt and clean trousers. That brought me back to the pain in my wrist. It would not go away. With every pulse my wrist throbbed.

I was soon back home. I had done well for myself in the past twenty-five years. My austere, but stately house, bespoke my position. What a far cry my residence was from some pest hole in Africa. As I stepped up upon my stoop a bit of brick crumbled and I lost my footing. I fell hard against the railing. Why must I suffer so? I closed the door behind me and climbed, with some effort, up the stairs to my room. There, on my ribcage, on the right-hand side, was an unsightly bruise. I ventured to touch it gently and was surprised at the pain. Perhaps there was some pain medication in the bathroom. in the cabinet above the sink. As I reached for the medication, I bumped the glass shelf. The shelf and its contents cascaded into the sink. My right hand held the pain medication so I reached into the sink with my left hand. another sharp pain, blood spurting from my left wrist. The jagged edge of the broken glass shelf must have cut a vein. I acted quickly, I wrapped a towel around my wrist, found gauze pads and tape. Soon, with pressure applied, the flow lessened and the flow eventually ceased.

I then became aware of more pain, this time in my feet. I looked down, saw blood spread across the bathroom rug and floor. In my pain, and in my haste to bind my wrist I had not been aware of the shards of glass upon the floor. Small cuts on both feet were spreading blood throughout the room. Why me, why must I suffer so unfairly. What a day this had been. Small band aids were enough to stop the blood. But perhaps there were splinters of glass inside the cuts. I had best see my doctor.

"Yes, could I be seen today, I had cut myself badly," I related to the voice on the telephone. "No, I could not come to the office," I said, "for I had cut my feet and thought glass splinters might have been driven in beyond my view. Okay, okay, send Dr. Freyling, if Dr. Galston could not attend." I did not really want to see a stranger. And how was I to get down to the front door to let this Dr. Freyling in? I soon heard knocking at my door. I opened the window and dropped my keys to the doctor. Why must it be a woman doctor? I never liked anyone to see me in pain, and especially a woman. It just wasn't seemly.

Soon however, she was up the stairs. Dr. Freyling was very efficient and methodical. Soon I was well bandaged. She checked the bruise on my chest and suggested I come in soon for an x-ray — possibly a cracked rib. She got me settled in my comfortable chair and said she would send round a pain medication.

"I can't leave you with such a mess, with glass all about the bathroom," she said sympathetically.

"It's no bother really, the maid comes on Wednesday anyway," I replied as stoutly as I could, though I did not feel at all well.

"No, you just risk more glass in your feet. Now tell me where your cleaning closet is, and I shall get to work."

I hadn't the strength to argue further, so I gave her directions. Soon she was back in my room. She picked up my dirty shirt, coat and tie and hung them on a hook in the closet. As she reached to pick up my shoes she gasped and picked up the newspaper instead.

"Are you okay?" I asked. "Oh yes," she responded, but it was clear that she was shaken by something on the front page. "It is this photo and story about my cousin. I have always admired her so. I too intended to be a missionary, to follow her to Africa. But after medical school I married a businessman." "But surely you live well don't you," I questioned?

"Oh yes, that's true enough, but she has done so much more, saved thousands of lives, while I have done so little." Then she looked up from the paper with some embarrassment. "I'm so sorry, I should not inflict my regret upon you. Come by the office on Thursday for a new dressing. Do you need this paper? Could I take it with me? "Certainly, you may have it."

Soon the pain pills arrived from the pharmacy and I began to feel their affect. Why did it seem like I was always the one who had to suffer? What a wretched day it had been.

Later, about 2:30 p.m., my client called to abuse me for having missed our appointment. Even after hearing a brief version of my afflictions, he criticized me for my carelessness and pressed upon me the inconvenience I had caused him. Some people have all the luck.

The Fool and the Wall

I sat down on the wooden bench, the one in the small garden behind the library. It was a pleasant day early in the spring, so I let my mind wander; I let the warmth of the sunlight penetrate my body. As I sat there, I felt good. I felt good because I am smart and prosperous, and it felt good to sit in the sun and be warm while others toiled. I heard the shuffling of feet along the path. Almost immediately I recognized whose footfall it was. I pretended to be asleep so that I would be left in peace, to sit here on the bench where the sun is warm and bright. But the footfalls ceased close to the gate.

He said, "hello my brother, how fortunate you are to sit there warmed by the sun, while others toil." But I ignored the one I sought to avoid and I did not answer.

But the fool, he did not go on, he waited. I began to get impatient when he did not leave. I cursed him silently. I cursed my ill luck to be trapped here, on the bench where I could not escape. There was only one gate and surely, he stood near it waiting for my reply. But I did not greet him, nor did I answer his greeting. Why should I talk to that old fool?

Yet he remained, there by the gate. I boiled with rage at him, willing him to shuffle on, to go wherever he usually went. Finally, I could take it no more. But I did not want him to know that I was intentionally ignoring him, so I pretended that a fly, or some other insect, had landed on my ear. I started up, as if suddenly awaken and beat the air about my face with my hands, as though afflicted by some noxious bug.

"Oh," I said "it is you. I have been napping here in the warm sun. Come, share my bench." I hoped he would not, I hoped he would tell me he had some place to go, but that isn't what he said.

"Sleeping?" He replied.

"Yes, here in the warmth of the sun, here in this small garden away from the traffic and noise." But he did not answer me as I expected, the fool.

"Would you open the gate?" He said somewhat distractedly.

"Surely you can open it yourself." I answered, somewhat curtly, so that he would know I wasn't prepared to take part in one of his idiotic games. You could never tell what he might say. There were times when he seemed to be in some other conversation. Surely, he could unlatch the gate for he was physically sound.

"Oh yes, the one to the garden, that one I can unlatch. But I mean the other gate, the one you seldom open."

What in heaven's name did the fool mean? What other gate? I had no gate where I lived. My door opened onto a small stoop, with stairs leading down to the pavement. What the devil is wrong with him? What sort of nonsense was he planning to put me through? For God's sake couldn't he just leave me here in the sun, on the bench. "Oh come now, what gate do you mean?"

"You know the gate, the one in the wall."

"Look, you are welcome here, but do not twit me with some fool's game. Open the gate yourself and enter the garden."

"Yes, I could come into this garden; I could come through this gate. Why not open the other gate? The gate you keep latched and locked, the gate with the rusty hinges."

The wall around the garden, here behind the library was barely waist high. He could easily hop or clamber over it if he did not want to come through the gate. Perhaps he was having some sort of vision or hallucination. It is likely that he had conceived that I was someone else, someplace where the walls were high and the gates were unused.

"Your gate is rusted shut, from disuse," he said, as if he had read my thoughts.

"Just clamber over the low wall, if the gate bothers you so, if you can't unlatch it yourself," I spat out.

"Ha!" He chuckled." I cannot lift a siege that has been clamped on from the inside out. Your battlements are manned. Oil boils in the cauldrons ready to be spewed upon any so foolish as to attempt to scale the high walls that enclose you."

"Look, you make me angry, I see no battlements, I see no cauldrons. I know you are prone to speak such nonsense, but do not think that I will listen to it."

"Oh yes," he spoke back quietly," I know that I am thought to be a fool and that may be so. But I could scale any wall, no matter how high, no matter how precipitous the climb might be, however I never force entry, I never use a battering ram for any gate, nor would I climb another's wall. I enter only through a gate or doorway that has been unlatched by the one who dwells within."

I was quite irritated by his drivel. What on earth did he mean? And why should I bother to care, for he is just a fool, a nobody. And I, I am a person of substance and some wealth. No one can have what I have attained without work, without some cleverness. Let the fool pass by; let him be gone. "Oh, the devil with you," I said, "enough of your foolishness. Either come through the gate or go along and leave me be."

"The devil indeed. So, you are aware of that much, at least."

"What has the devil got to do with it? Can't you leave me here alone in the sun." There I had said it. Maybe now he would leave.

"Yes, I shall leave, since you won't let me enter," he said as he bent down, perhaps to brush a sow bug, or some dust from his shoe. As he straightened back up, he spoke again, ever in that irritatingly calm voice of his, "when you open the gate for me, I will come.

Know that I will come when the walls become oppressive to you, when you want to be in the light and in the warmth."

Good God, what could he mean! Here I am sitting in the sun, warm and comfortable. Or at least I was until he came, intruding, badgering me with some idiotic nonsense about high walls and battlements. I was so lost in my thoughts that I did not hear him go, for I had turned away from him so he would not see the disgust my face held for him, for his kind. I closed my eyes, breathed deeply, in order to regain the calm I had lost, but it did not work. My mind churned, turned over the foolish phrases he had left with me, "I cannot lift a siege that has been clamped on from the inside out." What foolishness!

And now, wouldn't you just know this would happen. Clouds were moving in from the west, blotting the sun, leaving me to shiver on this bench. Why do I shiver? It is spring, but not so early in the spring. Oh, why did I let him unnerve me so? I rose hastily from the bench, stumbled across the uneven pavement and crossed quickly the small distance to the gate. The latch did not let go its hold until I beat my fists upon it. My knuckles began to bleed. I looked about to see if I were being watched. I stood there, finally outside the gate, to compose myself, so that nobody might guess the aggravation within me.

I strode once more, sure-footed along the narrow street. I greeted the baker as he swept the stoop before his shop. "Good day," I said.

"Oh yes, it is a fine day sir," he replied circumspectly.

I am sure he could not know the anger that seethed within me. Yes, he had better remain circumspect; I held the note for his shop. I could demand payment at any time. No one could touch me. I was sure to live a long and happy life.

Soon my steps had led me to my house. It was spare, not at all what you might expect for someone in my position. Yes, I did not need to care what the baker might think. He could not touch me. I bolted the door and closed the shade. How cold it was inside. I did not leave the fire lit while I was out—such a needless expense. But my feet were cold. I knelt to light the fire, which had been prepared by the maid. Through the chimney, for just a moment, I thought I heard the cooing of a dove. But wasn't it too early for that? No, it was just the wind. The same wind that drove the sun's warmth from me. Since the sun was now hidden by clouds, I shut the windows, latched them tight, and pulled the drapes shut. Now I could rest secure, wrapped in my blanket and sit in my chair. I was not expecting anyone to come. Entertaining was such a waste of time and money. Who needed all that senseless chatter let loose by a glass of wine or a four-course dinner? I would have a sandwich later, by myself.

Road Kill

There he was, standing at the edge of the roadway when I found him this morning. It appeared as though he were waiting for a break in the traffic to cross to the other side. He stood patiently beside a wooded section of road not far from the city limits. And yes, he did want to cross over; he did so when there was a break in the traffic. He appeared to be pushed forward by a sense of urgency. A shovel in one hand and cloth bag in the other, were his constant companions. I had not been able to see where he ducked through the hedge and into the wood, so I could not follow him further. Frustrated, after waiting for over half an hour for him to reappear, I returned home.

Yes, I had become obsessed. The focus of my obsession was a scruffy, and apparently homeless man with some very odd habits. My first thought was, that this man was one of the many that had been released from some psychological treatment center. And, no doubt, because of some psychological disability he was unable to find or retain employment. I had taken care not to call his attention to myself, but he seemed to sense that I was following him. And while he did not seem to mind my surveillance he did not, on the other hand make it easy for me to keep up with him. And, not knowing him any better than I did, I was reluctant to follow him closely, for he might have some propensity for violence and I did not wish to endanger myself.

It was early next morning that I first sighted him in the distance. He sat on a downed tree along the Bethesda Church Road, bag draped over the trunk, horizontal now, shovel at his feet. I leaned against a rail fence some fifty feet away so that I might observe him. He wore work boots, ankle height, rough denim trousers and a flannel shirt. His head was shaded by a cap, one that apparently touted some athletic club. After just a few minutes he rose and began to walk north along the road. His progress was steady, but not so fast that I could not keep up with him. Well, I do try to keep fit with regular walks and a sensible diet, low in salt and fat.

At the junction of Bethesda Church Road and Spring Hollow Road he stopped momentarily to let two cars and a delivery van pass by. Then he strode quickly across Spring Hollow and continued north on Bethesda Church. I had to wait several minutes before I could cross, and by that time he was far ahead. When he stopped again, he picked up his shovel and used it gently to remove something from the road and place it into the cloth bag. From my distance I could not tell what it was.

For several hours I followed him. Every so often he would repeat this action of using his shovel to pick up some object from the roadway and place it in his bag. But I was never close to him when he did this. Of course, this heightened my curiosity. I hurried to catch up with him, and though it was not a warm day I found my heart beating rapidly as a result of my efforts to close the distance. Then he disappeared again through a hedge. Yes, yes it was the same hedge as before, the one along the small wood on Cemetery Lane. I searched the hedge for some time, looking for passage through it, but could find none. Frustrated, I returned home for my lunch, quite exhausted.

All afternoon I thought about what I had seen. Then it occurred to me that he might have a camp or some rough shelter there in the wood. Instead of following him on his exhausting rounds I should seek out his camp. Then perhaps I might learn what he was about. Yes, that is what I would do.

Next morning, after my breakfast, I resolved to carry out my plan. It did take some time to find a place in the hedge where the branches parted when pushed. Once through the weak place in the hedgerow there were visible boot tracks through a boggy area. I must either go on ahead or turn back now, for this man would know that someone had found him out.

My curiosity propelled me forward and I did not travel far before I found a campfire ring with a pile of firewood nearby. There, within the remains of a shed I found his blankets, neatly rolled, and a small rucksack. Though I much desired to know what was in the rucksack I resisted the temptation to untie the cords and search the contents. I had already come where I had not been invited.

"Good morning sir," came from behind me. I was so startled that I almost fell on my face as I rose and turned to see who had spoken this greeting. It was him. He wore the same costume as before, though now I could see that the cap had inscribed upon it the word "Angels." He had with him the shovel and the cloth bag, bulging and apparently heavy with whatever filled it.

"Good morning," I replied somewhat circumspectly, as I was feeling embarrassed for intruding upon his private domain. "I apologize for my curiosity, but I have been wondering what is happening here."

"Yes, I know that you have been watching me," he replied, "are you working for the state?"

"Oh, I assure you my curiosity is private," I replied, and then I almost immediately regretted divulging the solitary nature of my quest. I feared momentarily that he might do me some violence.

"Then you may stay if you like, for I have nothing to hide," he replied as if no longer concerned. It was then that I noticed a wretched stench. At first, I thought it might be man himself. Perhaps he had not bathed for weeks. But no, it was not him, it was the cloth bag that stank.

"Yes, it is the bag," he said. "Come, follow along if you are curious." And without further words he placed the rucksack on his back and walked off down an almost invisible path through the wood. I followed him, but not so closely that the rank odor emanating from the cloth bag, would cause me to retch. How could he stand that smell, I wondered, as I followed behind him?

Soon we emerged into a small clearing. He placed the bag on the ground and gently, while wearing no gloves to protect his hands, he removed the corpses of small animals from the bag; opossums, squirrels, birds, frogs and what not. The enormity of these vile carcasses engulfed me and I fled into the tall grass and vomited all that my stomach contained.

When I returned to the clearing, for I could not suppress my desire to know what morbid objective drove him to such behavior, he was gently wrapping each carcass in clothes that he took from the bag. Without a word, he walked up a small incline to a rise in the clearing. It was then I noticed that there were hundreds of small wooden crosses spread over the grass.

With his shovel he slowly and carefully dug as many holes as there were wrapped bodies. He returned to the bodies, which he had prepared for burial and picked one up. He proceeded, with his burden in hand, to the first hole. He knelt by this small cavity, appeared to pray and then gently placed the body in its grave. He made eleven more trips up to the prepared gravesites, even though some of the wrapped bodies were so small that he could have easily carried several at once. I was amazed at the reverence he showed and at the care he took with each of the dead. It was as if he had known each of them. It was as though each was his true friend. It was when he returned for his rucksack that I noticed the tears streaming from his eyes. He was in deep mourning.

He climbed the small rise again to fill the holes. Then from the rucksack he took small crosses, matching those that already covered much of the rise. He placed one above each small mound, then knelt again in prayer. After some time, he sung a hymn. I was surprised for the hymn was sweetly sung and joyous, quite in contrast to his recent weeping.

I too had bowed my head while he knelt. Cautiously, I looked up again, but he had disappeared. I ran to the top of the rise, but he was nowhere visible. It was then that I could see the full extent of his cemetery. It spread over several acres of ground. I counted the graves. There were 2,871 in all. The poor fellow was obsessed. He must be totally crazy.

I returned home that evening unsure of what I should do. As I ate my sensible food and drank water instead of wine, I pondered what I had seen that day. I just did not know what to make of it. After reviewing my accounts, as I do each week, and reading for an hour, I went to bed.

It was that night that the dreams began. Each night for weeks thereafter I saw him empty the cloth bag and I saw the tears flow from his eyes. In my waking hours I began to fear that I too might be crazy, that I too might be driven to some odd behavior.

These dreams began to affect my waking hours, to interrupt me in the middle of meetings with my business clients. This could not continue or I would be ruined. I made an appointment with my doctor. I told him I had been having difficulty sleeping. He gave me a prescription and told me to get regular exercise.

I have followed his advice and now the dreams seldom return. I am so relieved.

Peace

Since I had read that newspaper article. Yes, the one in the Sunday paper, I had set a new course for myself. I would not let myself be consumed by the anger that filled so many. What was the good of conflict? Conflict had brought me no health, though perhaps some of my prosperity had come through conflict. But now I was prosperous so I need no longer drive myself; I must no longer stress myself for mere gain of wealth. Yes, I had decided that I might now ascend to the next level of being. I now planned to live at peace. And that is why I am here, sitting quietly in the church. No, don't begin to think that I am a believer. It has been clear for decades, if not longer, that the church knows nothing of peace. Yes, I shall sit and meditate, for here is the cool and calm, in this soft, morning light that filters through the pointed stained-glass windows.

There is no one here and the quiet is soothing. But the windows, some of the windows trouble me. There are images of dour saints staring down at me. Why must saints look so pinched, so sour and thin as though life has squeezed them dry. Oh, and that saint, the one bound to the column and punctured with arrows. How can that lead me to peace? This is not the place to find peace. The peace in this church is the peace of the dead, not of the living. I shall move to the garden, the one with the small fountain nestled in the cloister.

There are no sad eyes to stare down at me here, no dried-out men or women to curdle my serenity. I shall sit here, on this bench next to the fountain. These small flowers, sweet peas I believe they call them, they are cheerful and bright. Yes, I think solitude can be found here.

"May you go in peace."

"What, what? Is there someone here in the garden with me?" I had not seen anyone when I entered so I was caught off guard by this voice that sounded so near. I searched the small cloistered garden with my eyes but saw no one. Perhaps some joker, some fool was hidden in the shadows of the arched walkway surrounding the garden. Maybe someone was bending down, hiding behind a low hedge. I already felt somewhat foolish for speaking out, especially since I had seen nobody around. So, I rose slowly from the bench and stretched, acting as peace-filled as I could muster; then I began to amble about inspecting the plantings, the sundial, the bird bath. But I could see no one. I returned to the same stone bench, thinking I might nap, now that I had given up worldly struggle and conflict.

I had begun to nod, my eyes heavy with peace, for it was a fine summer day and there were only enough clouds in the sky to accent the bright blue above. It was then, when I had almost drifted into sleep, that it came again.

"May you go in peace," this time somewhat louder, somewhat nearer. I was so startled that when I sprung from my bench I tripped and fell. I skinned my knee on the pavement. There was even a small tear in my pants leg. I was determined to remain at peace, so I sat down again and breathed deeply, as the newspaper article had recommended. It did help somewhat, but I could feel anger rising within me. I was beginning to see that I would not remain composed and serene here in the garden so I decided to take my leave. First, I must have a destination. Otherwise I would fidget with agitation, uncertain as to how I should direct my steps. Without a goal I could not remain calm. Where could I find some soothing setting in which I could contemplate and focus my heart and mind?

"May you go in peace," the voice came again, even closer, but gentler than before. This time I held my emotions in check. I forced myself to sit. Others might be unnerved by such voices, but not I. I would not let such voices, no matter how soothing they might be, confound and defeat me, or drive from me my inner serenity. However, I did decide it might be best to do as I was bidden.

Having not determined a destination, I followed the path along the brook. I soon found that walking had its value. The brook made melodic, burbling sounds and wrens, of some sort, were flitting about in the hedges. And if I remembered correctly, the author of the article had recommended exercise. So yes, yes it was good to move, to walk at my own pace. And yes, I felt surface within me memories of following this path into a small wood long ago, when I was a lad. We had taken crude, handcrafted bows and arrows and hunted the sparrows and wrens, but without much success. I had, one summer day, managed to fell a sparrow. And after the small bird had ceased its ungraceful flopping about in the dust, I had approached it to glory in my marksmanship. But there was little glory to be found. For my rude arrow had pierced the sparrow's head. Blood dribbled from the wound and oozed over the feathers as they turned dull. To avoid the staring eyes of my fellows, I had run off along the trail and then hidden among the rhododendrons and vomited.

I caught myself. Surely such memories would bring me no calm. Shame had filled my eyes so that I could no longer see the flowers before me. Shame filled my ears and banished the sound of the brook from me. No, my past would bring me no peace. I must shove these thoughts from my mind.

"May you go in peace." This time I was not sure whether the words came from within or without. Was it my ears or my mind that perceived these same words? These words now seemed a cruel taunt. I know what peace is. Peace is freedom from conflict. I could live in peace as well as any other. By God, I'll show them. If anyone can be peaceful, I can. I have persevered in the past and reached my goals. And others, who thought they were smarter and stronger than I, they fell by the wayside. I left them in the dust. Yes, I had grown wealthy, I had been honored many times for my philanthropy; I could become a man of peace.

Now that I had a purpose I could act. I could set my course and follow it and not be distracted. I will have peace. I will have peace. I strode, confidently now, towards my office. It was on the first floor of my house. Why waste money on an office away from home. I climbed up the steps to the stoop, glancing momentarily at the white marble columns that flanked the door. They added just the right amount of solidity and dignity, without being overdone or ostentatious. I sat at my desk; my mind filled with ideas. As rapidly as I could I recorded my thoughts in my notebook. I organized them, rewrote passages that were unclear, and checked them over. Yes, now that my plans were outlined, I could begin.

"May you go in peace."

The voice was firm but audible. This voice was not some imagined hallucination. It was as real as the voice of my solicitor, that scoundrel. Then I heard the phrase repeating in my mind, over and over. I could not silence this seemingly, never-ending echo-like perseveration. Frustration and irritation began to consume me. Yes, I must take the sleeping pills. After sleep I would be rested, I could then find the strength inside myself to conquer whatever was plaguing me now.

My heart pounding irregularly as I lay in my bed. Thoughts raced within me; I could not master my thoughts. Yet I knew there was no one to help me. Who could you trust? My wealth, my status made it impossible for me to seek out advice from another. And even when I was young and more open to the proddings of another, I seldom found much that was useful in what they said. And now I knew of no one I could trust. Maybe I could go to another place, seek out the advice of a stranger. But how could I, a man of my position admit to not knowing how to proceed? How could I admit my failure? Surely a man of my abilities and cleverness should be able to find the peace I sought. Oh, to the devil with that newspaper article. I have no peace! I have no peace!

Next morning, after a night full of tossing and turning, I washed and dressed myself as usual - clean trousers to replace those that had been torn. In the restlessness of my night I had determined that to seek for peace was like seeking for love. Neither love nor peace are to be found in this world. I would return to my regular ways. They had served me well thus far; there was no reason to change now.

I breakfasted on tea and toast. I stick to simple fare. I see it as a virtue to do without the frills to which so many succumb. I put on my coat and hat, as usual, and set out for the exchange. I greeted the streetsweeper with "Good morning to you," even though he is a fool and a simpleton if there ever was one.

"May you go in peace," he responded, most respectfully.

I shot him an icy scowl and strode past him and greeted no one else that day with more than a curt nod. "Peace indeed!

Thirst

The sun beat down upon me with no mercy. Not even a bit of a breeze moved the parched air. Dust covered everything, my shoes, my trousers, my shirt, my tongue. My mouth screamed within the drought that encircled me. Let me find a place with shade in this vast treeless world of fields. I trudged onward, following the road as it curved southward and slightly uphill. All of me began to feel like cracked leather. My water had run out early this morning and I had not passed a well or stream since then. Yes, there had been the drainage ditch that ran fast and stinking before it passed through the culvert under this unpaved road. My lungs rattled dryly like parchment sheets before a fan; and to make it even worse, this morning, when I left my house, I had not put on my straw hat. The only moisture for miles must be the trickles of sweat that trace wet paths through the dust on my face and in along my scalp. Why had I worn my felt hat? Why had I forgotten to wear the straw hat? My skull baked as though in an oven.

Oh, where did she come from? Why on earth would she be here to torment me? Could she not be somewhere else tormenting someone else with her foolish prattling? "Good day ma'am," I said with all of the civility I could muster. I despised her there leaning against the fence wearing that light cotton dress, and looking so cool beneath that cheap straw hat. I was somewhat embarrassed for I was no longer wearing my coat and tie, as I usually do.

"Hello brother," was her greeting, as usual. "Do you mind if I walk with you for a while? I could use the company."

"Yes, I suppose you might as well," I said, attempting to blunt the sharpness of my reply.

"Notice how the waves of heat rise up from the fields, see how the grain prospers under the sun," she responded. Apparently, I had been able to disguise my displeasure at meeting her. My colleagues have often remarked at my coolness, at my ability to keep a poker face when negotiations are in progress. Yes, my reserve has been crucial to my prosperity. But what good was that for me here, as I perish now from thirst.

"Yes, the grain seems plentiful enough, it looks to be a good crop," I answered, but without enthusiasm. "Are there any wells close by, any place where one might get a drink?" I asked, almost pleading.

"Oh yes, I think there must be water about somewhere, for without it could the grain flourish so," was her answer. Did this woman not sweat? I hated her for her cool cotton dress, for her straw hat. If I had been less a gentleman than I am, I might have snatched her cheap hat and pushed her to the ground. She carried a small bag; it hung from a strap over her left shoulder. Maybe she carried a small canteen. But I could not ask. It is my rule to never seem to be in need. Need is a weakness, and I abhor weakness. I pick at other men's pathetic lives as a small boy might pick at a scab. I know how costly pain can be for others, and how much power and wealth it has given to me. Oh yes, I can exploit pain, and fear, and weakness and never shed a tear.

"Why are you walking today brother? Where is your car?" She asked quite innocently, or so it seemed. But her question was like a hot iron pressing on my lungs. I almost gasped, but caught myself in time.

"Well, if you must know, it broke down several miles back. I saw that I could remain with it and bake, or that I must follow this road to find a telephone or garage," I replied somewhat testily, for my thirst was punishing me. My lips were cracked now and it was painful to speak.

"Do you need water?" She asked, seemingly ignoring my barely suppressed hostility.

"Yes, I would very much like some water." I answered, trying the best I could to hide the urgency within me." Is there a stream or well nearby? If you know, please tell me."

"No, there are no wells and the streams have all run dry, but I have a small bottle of water in my bag." She spoke serenely, as usual, calm words flowing like a brook through the forest." You may have some for the asking, if you want."

Oh, I did want, I wanted with the whole of my being. But I could not ask. I must hide my need. My thirst was like a loose stone in a wall. If I let my thirst, my need be visible, my wall would collapse upon me and

I would die. I knew I would die for I had built my walls, the bastions of my ownership and power with the stones of other people's need and the mortar of other people's pain. If I allowed need to penetrate my walls I would be finished. Oh, how I hated her. If she would offer me a drink then I could accept. But to ask, no, I would go to hell before asking. If she had been a man, rather than a young woman, I might have found some way to wheedle an offer of a drink. Oh, now I do boil inside, for she has taken the bottle from the bag, and the water glints within the sunlight. I yearned so to taste the coolness on my tongue.

"I was going to take a sip myself," she said, "but I cannot if you will not. If you change your mind, there is water enough here to quench any thirst. Just ask when your thirst is sufficient."

"Oh, I could not ask," I flung the words at her, angry that she would tempt me so. I raged as she placed the bottle back in the bag and reclasped the clasp. As she adjusted the strap on her shoulder, I seethed. She lifted her hat to tuck stray hairs back in place and there was not a bead of sweat upon her smooth forehead. My scalp oozed sweat like a seeping spring and the rankness of my armpits was noticeable even to me. I felt so wretched. Why could she not just give me water, why must I ask?

It was then that I spied a narrow bridge over which our road must pass. It was not far ahead. In my thirst I raced forward, while with each panting breath I expelled the moisture from within me into the charred air. I noticed a small trickle in the creek bed. Now I would not need her bottle of water, no longer could she vanquish me with her placid face, wrapped in the shade beneath her straw hat. But how was I to get this water. This glistening trickle of water flowed through a deep and narrow rut, and neither my tongue nor lips could reach it.

As if sensing my dilemma, she offered: "I think I have a straw that you might borrow, if you wish it."

"Yes, I do wish it," I said, masking my need, my urgency, as much as I could. At least she had not forced me to ask. Wetness streamed into my mouth, my lips stung as if it were acid I sucked. My throat tightened. I gagged. This stinking trickle was laden with salt. I vomited back what I had so greedily swallowed.

"Is this water not to your taste?" She asked. The innocence within her voice searing me anew.

"Salty," was all that I could answer, for my stomach churned within me.

"Let me help you up," and she lifted me with a strength I did not expect from a woman. Soon I found myself leaning against the railing of the bridge. Her concern enveloped me and I felt my own weakness spread throughout my body. I was embarrassed, for I now appeared weak and helpless. I despise helplessness beyond all else, and now I was helpless. My thoughts were interrupted by her voice, "I do not have much further to go, would you like me to leave my water bottle with you, for I will not need it."

Her words pricked me like a scorpion's tail, for again she seemed bent on forcing me to ask for help. No, I could not do it. A man of my position did not ask women to help them. What would my colleagues say? Or, even worse — do, if I were to open my weakness, like a merchant displaying his wares, before this woman. I heard myself reply, "No, no I shall be fine, you have done enough already. I have troubled you enough already, and soon I shall be well enough to travel on."

"If that is what you wish she said. I would be happy to leave my water, to end your thirst, but since you want no water, I will go." She took several steps and then turned." If you thirst, I will come again to you. All you need do is ask and I will end this thirst you clutch so tightly."

Such impertinence, to accuse me so. "Oh please be off, go along on your way," I spat back, making no attempt to hide my annoyance. What nerve! I was in such a rage I did not see her go. It was almost as though she vanished into the fields of grain that engulfed all but the roadway. Perhaps the rising heat waves made it seem so. Anyway, I did not care.

Oh yes, I did get home. An old man came along in a truck. I paid him for a ride into town. I paid him for a bottle of water he had with him. That woman, she thought I might need her! What foolishness! Now, I sit here secure in my home. My fan blows cool air across my face. I have bathed and put on clean clothes. I have washed the stink of pigs from me, the stink that was imbedded in that old man's truck. He was a fool too. I would have paid him much more if he had asked. But he was too stupid, he never guessed my wealth until he saw my house and the name plate upon the door. Now I have all that I want to drink, cool tumblers filled with ice and water. The pain is receding from my lips, and soon I will be filled. I have finished three tumblers filled with water, and soon I will not want any more. Soon.

Interview with the Royals of Neo-Post-Arcadia: Queen Julian and King Narcosaria

By Donald Wrymouth

Cast List
DW – Donald Wrymouth
GP – Grand Poobah
QJ – Queen Julian
KN – King Narcosaria

(DW) First just let me say what an honor it is to be in your presence and have the chance to interview both of you. But before I ask my first question, I am somewhat confused about how I should address you. Queen Julian, should I address you as His Majesty Queen Julian? King Narcosaria, do I address you as Her Majesty King Narcosaria?

(GP) The truth is that you, being nobody of any significance, are not allowed to address either the Queen or King. Were you a person of significance you would then address the Queen as Sir? Monty, First Lady of the Royal Realm, and you would then address the Queen as Lady Cindy, First Knight of the Royal Realm. And you would do so without smirking, giggling or any other unseemly behavior. I, Felix Haugworth-Pettington-Twibly, Grand Poobah of the first order, will answer all questions. Of course either the Queen, or King, may respond at any moment; they are the Queen and King and thus free to not do whatever they wish to not undo and/or do not what isn't to be done not, whenever they should unpresume to do not whatever they do not do or leave undone.

(DW) Could you just explain your last sentence?

(GP) No!

(DW) How should I address you Felix Haugworth-Pettington-Twiby, Grand Poobah of the first order?

(GP) For now you can address me as Rrose.

(DW) Rrose then, where is Neo-Post-Arcadia?

(GP) Neo-Post-Arcadia is whenever and wherever the Queen and King decide it is. It always surrounds the royal persons including anything within 179 feet of their royal persons.

(QJ) You are presently in Neo-Post-Arcadia, even though you are an insignificant twiddling dingbat.

(GP) You must grovel and abase yourself whenever the Queen addresses you!

(DW) I kneel and kiss his painted toenails, then slap myself seven times.

(GP) Very well done, are you sure you were not born in Arcadia-Neo-Post?

(DW) Perhaps, given its somewhat vague location, it is possible. Those of us not dwelling in Neo-Post-Arcadia are aware that the Queen and King are celebrated patrons and advocates for the arts. Could you tell me about their love of the arts?

(GP) Yes, that is easy. They are both consummate artists. Queen Julian is a painter of crockery extraordinaire and King Narcosaria is a celebrated performance artist noted for her mockery.

(KN) I am the one who decides what is and is not art and my Queen decides who is and is not an artist!!

(DW) Rrose what are the criteria for art within the realm?

(GP) Don't address me as Rrose any more, instead address me as Handy Andy. As for criteria the King and Queen do not wish to be bound by any rigid, logical, rational or otherwise restrictive approach to criteria. Today the criteria for what constitutes art is: "that which does not too much resemble what was art prior to Wednesday last; and that which amuses us, tickles our fancy, offends the peons and bourgeoisie; and that which flatters the fads, fetishes and fictions of our present beloved affectations."

(DW) Do you mean to say that the criteria change according to the whims of the Queen and King?

(GP) Whim is considered to be a despicable and meaningless word, not to be spoken before the royals. Please rephrase your question using acceptable terminology.

(DW) Do you mean to say that the criteria changes according to the capricious notions of the royals?

(KN) This interview will cease if you continue to abuse our royal personages!!!

(GP) My not God! What will you not say! You must now

bemoan your stupidity and make known to the King how wonderful and wise she is. Now!!!

(DW) Handy Andy, would you please relay to the King, my utmost apologies. I am an ignorant outlander; I know not the ways of your enlightened Queendom, therefore I act the reprobate, the foolish profligate, the radiant narcissist; I am one who knows nothing, thinks not, one who lets the thoughts of the moment flow from my mouth without edits. Oh, please forgive me.

(QJ) If you continue to insult that which we admire we will throw you out this instant!!! I kneel and kiss his painted toenails, then slap myself seven times.

(DW) Oh how have I misspoken, please enlighten me Handy Andy.

(GP) Since August, the highest ranks within our realm have been bidden to seek after Narcissism; all editing is forbidden since it interrupts the babblings of universals that flow from the gut. Our two highest honors are Golden Ladyship of the Legion of the Profligate and also Anch of the Knights Reprobate Magisterium Excelentius.

(DW) How then should I appropriately bemoan my stupidity?

(GP) That is simple, you must say "I, Donald Wrymouth, do solemnly swear that I have studied art history, philosophy, theology and various arcane disciplines that have imprisoned me within the narrow-minded penitentiaries of knowledge, reason and insight. I now eschew logic, empathy, morality, ethics, religions of all manner except for those currently allowed. I do honor you for your vapid mindset, your ability to agilely frolic with unwitting glee from moment to moment free of all mental, spiritual and ethical constraints that might limit in any way your ability to embrace or reject whatever might provide you with royal pleasure." It is quite simple.

(DW) *(I did repeat what Handy Andy suggested. Both King and Queen then smiled warmly upon me again.)*

(QJ) Well done! Well done! You may continue with your questions.

(DW) How often are the criteria for acceptable art subject to revision?

(GP) There is no set schedule. The royal personages have indicated to me that they might institute new criteria next Friday at 3:15p.m (N-P-AST). However, that is dependent upon the production of the royal pottery breaking factory. Since everyone was fired last week for not providing a sufficient amount of shards. The new criteria will also be somewhat dependent upon the art presented by the Queen and the performance piece that are to be presented at 3:23p.m., that same day. The current criteria have been in effect for 228 hours and 29 minutes. Before that, Criteria #847 decreed that all art, musical, visual and theatrical, and including arts that do not fit these hide-bound categories, was to be veiled in the raiment of emotive, aleatory and emphatic non-redundancy.

(DW) What kind of artistic response did Criteria #847 engender?

(GP) Very good, you are learning to ask questions that allow for the necessary ambiguity of critical response. Nonetheless, the artistic response was, as it is in response to all royal dictates, immensely positive. Queen Julian broke the plates himself rather than leaving that to an acolyte. King Narcosaria performed aleatory verse in response to the Queen's rhythmic and unpremeditated crockery breaking. It was a critical success as well. *NeoartNews*, *PostArt in America, and NeoPost Forum* all responded with ecstatic praise.

(DW) Is there ever any response to the art of Neo-Post-Arcadia that is not exaltation soaked?

(GP) Well of course in our Queendom we do not subvert the freedom of the press. However, some publications such as *ArtTweek* and *BurlyDame Magazine* ceased to be allotted royal licensure. But that had nothing to do with their somewhat obtuse critical stance; it was merely over technical issues related to non-compliance with Graphic Design Directive #1193. I believe that it involved the use of an unauthorized font, Times New Roman if I remember correctly, and I usually do (see Font Decree #863 for details). So, to answer your question less ambidextrously, the left hand does clap the right hand when applauding the freely sanctioned art of our current crop of artistic tyros. We are proud of the ceaseless energy, the unrestricted ideation and tolerance for tripe that our newly-minted artists incorporate in their ecstatic, enterprising and bombastic flow of inconsequential but deeply personal artistic effluvia.

(DW) No doubt, if I may ask Handy Andy, the term effluvia, as you use it, is complementary rather than pejorative.

(GP) Don't address me as Handy Andy anymore; from now on address me as Basquiat. I suggest in future you do a better job of researching the backgrounds of those you plan to interview. The most recent edition of our Queendom's dictionary is available online at www.Neopostarcadia/dictionary/#584. If you make use of this essential resource you will find yourself apprised of the status of words. Further, if you find a word to be un-present in the latest edition of our national diction-ary, you will remind yourself that its omission is entire-ly not unintentional.

(DW) I shall immerse myself in that resource as soon as the need re-presents itself.

(KN) I caution you. We are not brainless twits, though when called to we can enact those roles with great aplomb; we recognize irony when we see it.

(GP) You must insult and abase yourself before the King!

(DW) I kneel and kiss her painted toenails, then slap myself seven times. The King grimaces (unfortunately allowing some sort of salad green to become visible. No doubt some spinach or watercress has become impaled on her left lower incisor).

(GP) Donald Wrymouth you are indeed an idiot; one does not treat King and Queen alike.

(DW) I am so sorry; I acted as I thought I should. Please forgive my ignorance.

(GP) More insults!! The Queen and King do not forgive,

"for to forgive is divine," and the Queen and King are eternally and most emphatically and atheistically non-divine. However, they are supreme. Do you wish to continue?

(DW) Yes, most surely. What must I do to be absolved?

(GP) First you must stop using religious terminology!

(DW) At once; I am ever ready to comply Basquiat!

(GP) When you have offended the King, you must immediately knock your head against the floor three times and then slap yourself on your rump seven times. One is not allowed to touch the King.
I complied with these directions. However, the King continued to frown, the King did not seem satisfied.

(GP) She is royally miffed, ticked off and aggravated. You did the wrong rite; I just wanted to see if you would do anything I told you too. Have you no pride at all? The correct rite, not the wrong rite, consists of kissing the sole of each of the King's feet seven times, then slapping your forehead six times.

(DW) But dear Basquiat, I am not allowed to touch the King.

(GP) Right you are, for you should be in the wrong if you had followed my instructions. At least you have proven that you are not a totally brainless ninny. To abase yourself properly you must kneel, kiss the floor six times and then clap your hand fourteen times.
I followed these instructions explicitly. The King, who had been snickering behind her fan, did indeed seem mollified

upon the completion of this performance.

(DW) May I ask which artists are currently favored by the Queen and King?

(GP) Yes. Yes, you may. Keff Joons is the very favorite, for the Queen loves giant bunnies. The Royals have given Joons the official title of Chancellor of Cliché, Tyro of Tacky! His work is greatly beloved by all who dwell in Neo-Post Arcadia. The Royals are also extremely fond of Ohris Clifi. Clifi has been appointed Grand Flinger of Elephant Dung Third Class and awarded the Plastic Scarab; the order of the Plastic Scarab alone is considered a high honor in Arcadia-Neo-Post. Only the Macramé Spider's Web of Fate outranks the Plastic Scarab. Such awards as these are reserved for the most exalted of artists. Queen Julian himself has been awarded three MSWF's and fourteen PS's. King Narcosaria has been awarded four MSWF's, six PS's and been honored with a one-of-a-kind award the Ham-Fisted Galoot Extraordinaire. Queen Julian is hoping eventually to receive a H-FGE or some other equally prestigious award in the near future.

(DW) I'm sure that he will not be disappointed.

(GP) In that you are correct. King Julian and Queen Narcosia have reached the state of total emborement, thus this interview must cease. Good bye.

Sleeping Through the Apocalypse and other Unpleasant Occurrences

When I realized that I had spent the whole night playing on-line video games it hit me. It was actually my wife's pillow that hit me. "Calm down over there," came from the other side of our individually regulated king-sized air-master bed. Her dulcet-toned voice oozing with sarcasm brought it home, more than anything else. My world had become totally sugarcoated. My pondering the state of the cosmos—with me at the center—which was only fitting, was rudely interrupted, by the nasty, high-pitched buzzing of my alarm clock. As I scrambled to reach the off switch I heard, or at least I thought I heard a vaguely Native American voice reciting an age-old tale of the birds singing the sun into being each morning. It was then I knew, I mean I knew for certain, that I had no clue; I hadn't the foggiest idea of who I was or where I was. I had to acknowledge that if I had a diary, which I don't, that all of the pages would be blank. Nothing, absolutely nothing about my life was real; I was bereft of authenticity.

Though I might have consumed the milk of human kindness when I was young, it was certainly not what filled me any more. I suspected that if I were brought before the throne of God Almighty, which I hoped would not occur soon or unexpectedly, that instead of hearing the sonorous tones of a God who spoke with a voice resembling that of James Earl Jones, I would hear a voice closer to that of Judge Judy. And my fear of Judge Judy, I know now, was symptomatic of a much larger problem. My problem was that I needed more time. I could no longer keep up with the annoying demands of work, office politics, the boring and offensive habits of my colleagues, especially Dennis whose office was across the hall from mine. Every day he would provide me with his daily sports update. I became convinced that the recurring nightmare, of his play-by-play recap of his son Danny's and his daughter Daisy's sporting careers, would force me to take an interest in semiautomatic weapons. Again, I find that I have wandered away from my point, the one about needing more time. Maybe I could sleep less. No that was out, for I found myself wanting to nap at about 2:30p.m. every day as it was. If the boss found me napping I would be fired, and that would really foul up my life.

Some of the musings recounted above happened over breakfast, which consisted of yogurt and granola chugged down as quickly as possible. Then there was showering and shaving, all part of the tedious routine prior to work. Then came the drive, usually about forty-five minutes, to the office. I usually listened to public radio news because it was the least offensive. Unfortunately, during the boring parts of the drive, or about 99% of the time, I had time to muse and think about my life. As always, musing was a dangerous way to spend my time. Unwanted and obnoxious thoughts tended to intrude uninvited. For example, last Thursday I got to thinking about the role of crows in the universe. Crows, ravens, rooks, corbies, or whatever they are called, seem to provide no useful services to the universe. Yes, they can quoth, like the one Poe mentions; they help scour the streets and avenues of road kill, but they are not alone in this. They are always squabbling like politicians or university professors; it's always "much ado about nothing" so to speak. In recent movies they seem to either represent evil or act as agents of evil. Some mornings, especially in summer, they are up and about making a racket prior to the time my alarm clock is set to end my slumber. Then there was the time when my dreams were filled with a Native American voice, telling about the battle between the crows and the warblers. In this ancient battle, before mankind came to upset the balance of nature, the crows fought to displace the sun with eternal night and the warblers called endlessly upon the radiant sun, pleading for it to remain always high in the sky. In the end Tawamanda, the ruler of the heavens and maker of the universe, settled upon a compromise. In the end Tamawanda divided the days between light and dark by making the earth spin as it traveled through the heavens. Of course I tried to find out who this Tamawanda was without success. Other than a Boy Scout camp in southern Missouri, Google seemed clueless. Clearly the collective unconscious has a few glitches, if the voices within my dreams cannot be verified within my times of consciousness.

Oops, I find that I am sitting, unaware of my surroundings, in a parking place behind the building where I work. The motor is running, the voice of a reporter with an odd accent is relating some political news from Ivory Coast. As I look up into the rearview mirror, I notice two of my colleagues talking and gesturing; I'm pretty sure they are wondering how long I will remain in my car. I have overhead snippets of conversation about my unique behavior. I have no memory of my drive beyond the intersection of Doobler Street and Vibitz Avenue. All too often this seems to happen, I space out and have no conscious memory of where I have been and of what I have been doing. In order to divert attention from my colleagues, I pretend to be talking on my cell phone. They begin to move towards the door, so maybe the old cell phone ploy has succeeded after all.

I've asked my doctors about my lack of remembrance, but all they can recommend is the latest clone of Prozac. Or, they would be happy to recommend a psychologist or a psychoanalyst, but I'm not about to follow that path. Maybe I should go see that Naturopath, Dr. Schlemeny, I think it was, who had a knack for helping people with a dietary imbalance get their eating under control. So, I ate too many cookies; how could that affect my memory? Somehow I found myself at my desk, halfway through a package of Oreos. I made a quick trip to the restroom to rinse the Oreo crumbs from my mouth. There's nothing worse than smiling into a mirror and finding dark crumbs stuck between your teeth. Actually there are many things that are much worse, like acid rain and acid rock, but you do understand how embarrassing it could be to break into a smile with obvious dark speckles on a field of white—okay, ecru.

I know, I know, all I seem to do is ramble. I never keep on topic. However, in my own defense, I did mention that my world had become totally sugarcoated. So, I have at least returned to the topic of sugar. My life seems directionless, as though I am always getting distracted, diverted from some intentional focus. It is as if I live in a Hallmark Card universe where everything is pleasant, but nothing is ever important or significant. I shy away from any type of confrontation with almost everyone I know. So how do I get a real life? Or maybe I need to ask myself; do I want to get a real life? Sometimes I think I want a real life, then at other times I am pretty certain that a real life would be more painful than I could bear. I don't watch the news or read the news; the newsreader enunciates the worst disasters looking beautiful or handsome and wearing a disgustingly smarmy smile. How can they smile and update the body count at the same time? I sometimes find it difficult to live in this world where the media wants me to believe almost everything, while telling me at the same time that I should question everything.

Take, for instance, Yahoo's presence on the Internet. When I go on line Yahoo posts links to websites obsessed with the poor style decision of some actress starring in a third-rate sit-com. Why anyone should care about this is beyond my comprehension. Along this same line, is there anyone who can explain, in some truly rational way, what it means when Yahoo alleges "trending Bob Noodleman?" I have wondered how one trends or if I occasionally trend without being aware that I am doing so. Is it really believable that a major business entity, like Yahoo, could not make better use of the "wonderful" technological advancements of the past decade? When I contemplate the inanity of it all I begin to crave more cookies; I want to drown my skepticism with a binge of sugar and carbs. The same site links me with world news, usually focused on the latest mayhem or natural disaster. Don't these geniuses know that images of blood-lust, carnage and toppled houses makes it difficult for me to sleep securely at night and concurrently make it more likely that I will pig out on chocolate chip waist expanders?

Am I supposed to believe news reports posted by the same website that has links to horoscopes, videos of dancing Chihuahuas and news of the paranormal? I don't think so. My colleagues, if you can append such a label to my coworkers, think I am a bit loco because I am bothered by such inanity. They never understand why I have no interest in brackets when March Madness is their current sports obsession. For me brackets are pieces of metal used for supporting cheap bookshelves made of sawdust, glue and a paper veneer. They accuse me of being some kind of elitist, pinheaded liberal pimple on the butt of the body politic.

My coworkers seem to spend their weekends affixed to their lazy-boy loungers, eyes glued to a screen that displays the moving images of athletes attempting to do something with sporting equipment. They don't all belong to the same sect of the religion of sports. Some worship basketball, other baseball while most seem to believe that watching football, whether professional or college, will help them live a vital and meaningful life in a universe that is otherwise confusing and indecipherable. While I spend my weekend hiking, my favorite form of penance for my sin of obesity, they stuff chips into their mouths and/or swill some brand of alcoholic beverage, or perhaps high fructose infused fizzy drink. Can such a universe actually exist? I truly think that I am living in a dream world concocted by some sadistic and demonic science fiction writer.

Okay, maybe I don't live in a grade B movie scenario. So, thinking speculatively for a moment, if I don't act and react according to the dictates of some demented author, why does the world I live in always seem on the verge of total chaos? Maybe on the "verge of total chaos," is a bit limp and weenie-like. For the world seldom seems merely on the verge, it seems to be swirling wildly in preparation for being sucked into the sewer of eternity. More often than not I look forward to the sewer of eternity; it could easily be preferable to the inchoate present. I mean, every day I would really like a map that would provide the guidance I need to get through my day without severe and irreparable damage to my admittedly fragile psyche. Yes, I know I could always click on that link to the horoscope page. I have tried that. But instead of guidance my on-line seer postulates, and apparently with all due seriousness, a huge load of fertilizer, which unlike steer manure, has no nutritive value. I have even, although only briefly, turned to televangelists for guidance; they too seem bent on providing fertilizer. The only difference is that they ask me to send money, so that they may continue their essential on-air ministry. If their coifs are a reliable indicator, it looks like they merely want enough funds to keep them in good stead with their favorite Baroque hair salon or their wig-makers.

Here again I find that I am wandering off-track. Or, maybe in truth (whatever that is) I begin to believe that there is no track to be on. Maybe everything is just aimless, unimportant and stupid as the nihilists suggest. By the way how come some nihilists go to so much trouble to convince me that life and the universe make no sense, and that there is really nothing worth doing? So, if nothing is worth doing, why do they work so hard to convince me that this is the case? But then as I reflect, which I make every effort to avoid, why should I care what the nihilists do; let them act in ways contrary to their philosophy. In fact, if nothing makes sense how could anyone, even some pansy of an intellectual, bother with philosophy? I mean, having a philosophy would seem to require some interest in rational thinking, and even worse, reflection.

I feel the need for a new infusion of sugar arising from deep within my soul. Oops, I have used the word soul, and this is not currently politically correct for it implies at least some kind of spirituality or religious connection.

Gosh, I just noticed my supervisor heading my way, so I will need to switch over to another file that appears to be work-related. There is something about her demeanor that indicates I may be in for a good scolding. I know, I know the Fitzgerald account needs to be brought up-to-date.

Whew, she walked past my cubicle to Tony's cubicle. I hope he saw her in time to switch from the most recent on-line computer game to some kind of work-related document. Tony and I don't see eye to eye. For one thing he is seven inches taller than I am. Tony is a computer geek of sorts. He spends his time in one of two ways when in his low-end apartment. He is either scanning the web to see what's new in the world of computer techy geekdom, or he is defeating someone or something on-line in some virtual world, a world where everything operates according to geek-think. I can at least commend Tony for having absolutely no interest in watching or hearing about some recent sports event.

The way I figure it, in relation to professional athletes is, those people make a lot more money than I do, so why should I pay some outrageous price to watch rich people stuff a ball through a hoop or swat tennis balls over a net. I have no doubt that these athletes are skilled, but why should I pay what is big bucks for me to sit on a hard bench among people I don't know and probably don't want to know. I can say one positive thing about sports; it isn't merely virtual reality. It most likely isn't entirely real either, but that's a separate issue.

Whoa, it's five minutes into my lunch break and here I am on another trek into Dave's world, a place I spend too much time in. It's time for the old PB&J on white bread and a soda. Most of my fellow office workers have escaped to one of the nearby fast food emporia to purchase, as Dennis likes to say, a gut bomb. So I feel virtuous. No, not because a PB&J is a virtuous meal recommended by your friendly dietician, but because it's cheap. I'm saving up for a new SLR type digital camera. At the rate I'm saving money by staying in for lunch; I will be able to afford the camera and accessories I want in a mere 4,237 days. Boy, that is way too depressing to think about! I guess its back to the computer to solve on-line crossword puzzles for me. Such ecstasy can be found almost nowhere else online.

Lunch hour and the excitement of crosswords puzzles made it feel as though time was racing by at snail speed. Why can't I have a job I really enjoy, a job that provides me with an adequate amount of money and also gives me a positive reason to get up in the morning? Oh yes; now I remember. I majored in art; what else is there to say. Actually quite a bit, but I would rather express myself through linocuts or acrylic paintings. I'm not really all that excited about being a flunky in an insurance office. My hours are spent joyously; I enter data and review data and send out updates and information about how you are well served by your current coverage. However, you may wish to consider the advantages of altering your insurance coverage in the following ways, etc. etc. ad infinitum, amen.

I'm sorry for that mini-rant; a cyclone of self-pity carried me away. What can I say? Art majors are supposed to go for the gusto. Well, in truth that's what the beer drinkers seek, or so the advertisement would have us believe. I tend to have these bouts of self-pity several times a week, especially during the darkest days of November through March, a period of the year designed by sadists no doubt. If, in my spare time, which I usually spend raking leaves, unclogging ancient plumbing and changing light bulbs in electrical appliances, I get to pursue art instead of the above-mentioned methods of self-torture, I make art. Art has slipped from the back burner to a pilot light—it burns dimly.

I have another additional impediment to making art and her name is Jessica. Jessica is my spouse. She too would prefer that I aspired to greater things; she wants me to earn more money so that she can pursue her redecorating ambitions. Unfortunately, Jessica majored in Interior design. After graduation she discovered to her dismay that twenty-three million other women also majored in interior design. So instead of heading up a major interior design salon she is currently employed part-time to stock shelves at the neighborhood Piggly Wiggly. This has left her unfulfilled, and that is something I can understand down to the depths of my very soul. However, her minimum wage employment does not allow her funds for interior design on the grand scale to which she aspires. Needless to say, funds are scarce for both of us. Thus, when there is time for art, I must approach it in a miserly fashion. So, instead of large expressionist paintings, I am reduced to creating small drawings. I use high quality paper so I must limit my output to two drawings a month. I allow myself the luxury of matting and framing two drawings per year. I can hardly bear to reveal the soul-wracking, gut-wrenching embarrassment that results from these limitations to my creative persona. Needless to say, whenever I contemplate my dismal situation—and the almost universal rejection of my works by local galleries—I despair. So many philistines and sycophants, and no collectors with the courage to stretch their arms and draw unto themselves my insightful and evocative images that fill this mortal realm. I can see now that I shall soon be too dispirited to do anything other than watch some sort of inane reality TV program. And that will only serve to drive me deep into a grand funk that could last for days or weeks. We live in a soulless world without the least scrap of justice.

The Great Birdhouse

Many people came each day to see the birds and the changes that were made to the great birdhouse. In one large cage of the great birdhouse there were many fat chickens; some laid brown eggs and some laid white eggs. The chickens were always happily clucking, eating and enjoying their spacious light-filled room and had many keepers to look after them, so they were very comfortable. The people who came to the birdhouse were impressed with the fat, lively and productive chickens.

Not far from the wing where the chickens resided, was another large wing with many singing birds and there were a multitude of keepers who looked after the singing birds. Some sang sweet, lyrical songs and some twittered simple folk songs, while the mocking birds improvised. The wing for singing birds had countless cages and passageways between them. Lights and elaborate microphone systems were mounted so that different singers could be spotlighted.

In another large wing of the bird house, soon to be replaced by a newer and even more up-to-date structure, there were birds that could count, make complex machines whiz and whir and make liquids gurgle and bubble. Some visitors liked these birds best, for they made complicated actions look easy. There were plenty of keepers to take care of the machines and feed these smart birds.

In yet another wing there were the praying birds. As befitted these spiritual aviators, their surroundings were more ascetic and sparse. But nonetheless, there was an abundance of room for prayer and meditation, acapella singing and preaching. These birds often offered to share their food with their human visitors. Visitors to this wing usually went away feeling less burdened by the woes of the world. Many keepers took care of this spiritual wing of the great birdhouse.

Down the hall there were the talking birds. Parrots that could recite entire plays by Synge and Mynas that could offer critiques of poems by Elliott and Pound. For the children, parakeets narrated The Tales of Narnia and The Giving Tree. Several keepers trained these eloquent birds, fed them well and prompted them when they forgot their lines.

Far away, at the end of a dark and narrow hallway was a large, dim and dingy room, once used for the smart birds. There was one small cage and in the cage were many dark and iridescent birds. If there had been more lighting or daylight, the iridescent feathers would have looked beautiful and visitors could have gotten a better view of the tiny and colorful eggs in the small nests. Very few visitors liked this room, for it was dim and cold. The birds got whatever food the chickens, singing birds, smart birds, talking birds and spiritual birds did not want. There was only one keeper and he took care of these birds along with a gallery of bird art.

In most wings of the great birdhouse there were guided tours. The keepers took turns as tour guides and rested between tour groups, while the keeper of iridescent birds acted as guide to all visitors who came to his large, dim room at the end of the hall. So, when visitors filled out their bird house surveys before they exited, only a few had good things to say about the iridescent birds in the large, dim, and dingy room. They did not sing beautiful songs, produced nothing good to eat, did not recite, or act smart, or spiritual. Many of the keepers who worked in the birdhouse wanted to get rid of the iridescent birds; wanted to replace them with something more useful, more high-tech, more modern. For some reason, the iridescent feathers were not visible in dim light and the small colorful eggs did not measure up. The iridescent birds knew that they were not popular enough, so they grew sorrowful and disappointed.

Decades ago, when the birdhouse was built, the architect saw to it that every birdhouse was provided with just what it needed. The owls were given a dark room since they liked the night and cardinals were given sunflower seeds, which they especially liked. Woodpeckers were given rooms with high ceilings and tall trees upon which they could pound their beaks. The keepers of the birds were given what they needed as well.

It was when the visitors began to come into the great birdhouse that things began to change. There were visitors who liked some birds better than others; some visitors liked flamingos better than crows and chickens better than wrens. The more popular birds were eventually given more room, more food and more toys than the less popular birds. The architect's plans were forgotten and the visitors and keepers remodeled the great birdhouse according to the latest fads, fashions and whims.

Day after day the mute iridescent birds languished in their sorrow. The visitors still came to see them, but now they mocked these dark and silent birds. Visitors ridiculed the birds; they railed at them because in their sadness, the iridescent birds no longer laid the tiny colorful eggs.

Then one day, a young man came into the dim room of the iridescent birds; just before the room was set to be demolished. He fed the birds a special treat of nutritious dogwood berries and the birds gave up their sorrow. Once the birds' spirits were revived, the young man set to work with saw, hammer and drill. He worked all night until the dawn of the next day.

With morning, bright light flooded in through new windows and skylights. The light reflected off of mirrors, yellow and white walls, as well as colorful carpets and tapestries. The iridescent birds sparkled and blazed in their cages. In every nest lay tiny colorful eggs, bright and shiny like polished gems resting in neatly woven nests. The young man hired more keepers to tend to the birds. When this task was finished, the young man set to work on the other wings of the great birdhouse. When the great birdhouse was restored to its original design, the birds in every cage, every room, and every wing flourished. Visitors came from far and near; exit surveys were no longer needed now that the restoration of the great birdhouse provided everything the birds needed to prosper.

Acknowledgements:

Thank you to the following people who contributed to this book:

Amber Kirkwood, for her help editing, publishing and book cover design for Tree Story, Turning Radius and Parables Ironic and Grotesque.

Jay Beaman, Karen Bowdoin, Lynn Fox, Mark McLeod-Harrison for taking the time to read and review this work.

Anthony Kuenzi for his help with creating the book cover layout and design files and manuscript formatting.

Alphagraphics for adding page numbers and manuscript formatting

---

Other books by Douglas G. Campbell:

Tree Story. **(Portland, Oregon: Oblique Voices Press, 2018)**

Turning Radius. A Book of Poetry. **(Portland, Oregon: Oblique Voices Press, 2017)**

Facing the Light: The Art of Douglas Campbell. **(Portland, Oregon: Oblique Voices Press, 2012)**

Parktails. **(Eugene, Oregon: Wipf and Stock Publishers, 2012)**

Seeing: When Art and Faith Intersect. **(Lanham, Maryland: University Press of America, 2002)**